The
Seduction
of Sarah

Jacki Bishop
Early Riser Publishing

Publication Page

Seduction of Sarah
by Jacki Bishop
©2015 Jacki Bishop. All rights reserved.

ISBN: 978-0-9905315-6-2 (Paperback Version)

Early Riser Publishing
P.O. Box 711
101 E. Baltimore Ave.
Media, PA 19063
www.JackiBishop.com
jaxstir@gmail.com

Disclaimer:
The characters and situations in this story are
fictional, a product of the writer's imagination.

Cover Artwork: Andrii Ladik |Dreamstime.com

Cover Design: Rik Feeney / www.RickFeeney.com

Books by Jacki Bishop

The Seduction of Sarah

Death Sentence

Sarah's Gone Missing

The Seduction of Sarah

"I'd be more comfortable if you had a weapon," said the judge.

"What?" Sarah asked, wheeling around to face him. "Dad, you know how I feel about guns!"

"Of course I know how you feel. But I want to know I've done everything I can to ensure your safety in a new place, far from home," he answered.

Sarah didn't answer immediately, thinking this was probably the closest her father could come to expressing his love, convoluted as it was, and disguised as concern for her safety. Or perhaps he just needed to do what he felt was responsible.

"OK, Dad." Sarah caved. "But I don't know squat about using a gun."

"I've planned for one of my marshals to give you lessons; I'm sure you'll pick it up quickly. Andrew Milano can give you your first lesson this afternoon.

By the way, he'll also be driving you to school on Sunday."

Sarah was stung by the off-hand way he'd delivered the news that he wouldn't be taking her. She always wanted more from him than he could give. She'd have to lower her expectations, she thought with regret.

"Sarah"" her father asked. "Is something wrong?"

What could possibly be wrong, she thought bitterly. What she said was, "Dad, I still have packing to do." She turned away as he left the room. She didn't want him to see her tears.

Her thoughts spiraled downward. Graduating from Columbia in the top third of her class, in Poli Sci, no less, had failed to elicit the praise she yearned for. When it came to choosing a law school, she'd said, *fuck it*, and decided to go to Widener, in Delaware, instead of applying to her father's school, Yale. It was probably the first time she'd defied him. He was no doubt still pissed about her decision, but it didn't matter; going to Yale wouldn't have made them bosom buddies, anyway.

She'd spent the summer in Branford, hoping they'd grow closer, but that hadn't helped either. She'd all but given up on the relationship, so it was time to break away and go farther from home to start with a clean slate.

Sarah had amassed enough money working for a year on the stock exchange, and investing wisely, to make her feel financially secure. She would, however, accept financial help from her father.

Sarah had finished packing for the time being; she left the room to meet with the marshal.

***

On Sunday Sarah was ready to leave for law school. Her father had come in to say good bye early in the morning. Evidently he was on his way to the office, where "a mountain of briefs" were waiting for his attention. She told herself that once again, her father was immersing himself in work to avoid any unwarranted emotion. That was the reality and she had to accept it.

Andrew Milano, one of the Federal marshals protecting her father, arrived at ten A.M. to drive her to Delaware. Sarah put the earbuds in and listened to her iPod to avoid awkward conversation during the drive. Marshal Milano was a nice man. He had been kind and patient while teaching her proper handling of a gun. But she felt it would be easier on both of them for her to emotionally remove herself for the duration of the trip.

Sarah had packed a lunch for them and they stopped for gas outside of NYC, eating in the car. The rest of the trip passed quickly and they were in Delaware before she knew it.

Pulling up outside of the apartment building, Sarah was glad she didn't have to contend with the moving-in, saying 'Goodbye' ritual that marked the opening of undergraduate school. While part of Widener University, the law school was in Delaware, the main campus was in Pennsylvania.

Her father had, in fact, accompanied her to Columbia her freshman year. Even though they'd had a strained relationship, at least he'd come to help her move in. But, she told herself, *I'm an adult now and have to fend for myself.* Actually, it would be much like boarding school, but she was older now.

Milano helped carry all of Sarah's belongings in and, when she was moved in, offered to take her to dinner. She was about to decline his kind offer, but changed her mind as she contemplated spending an entire evening alone in a new place, with none of her familiar things around her. Her father had found her a furnished apartment.

During dinner they talked about ordinary things. Milano shared with Sarah what his first year of law school at The University of Pennsylvania was like. She'd heard the same story from nearly everyone she knew; first year was a bitch.

As they finished dinner, Sarah grabbed the check and insisted on paying for dinner.

Walking back to the car, Milano asked Sarah if she thought she could get around without a car.

"I thought I'd wait and see if I need one. If so, I'll get one here in Delaware; no state tax."

"That's smart, Sarah," Milano said. "But your dad does have that Camry sitting in his garage; he has me take it out occasionally just to keep it running. I'm sure he'd be willing to give it up."

"I don't like to ask my dad for things if I don't absolutely have to," Sarah said. She was afraid she sounded callous, so she added, "You know, being an adult."

"Sure, I understand," Milano added, as they arrived at the car.

When he left, Sarah felt alone, abandoned. She took a long bath and pondered her new situation. What advice would her mother have given her, she wondered. Thinking of her mother gave her a feeling of connection. And she knew what advice her mother would've given her, "Shake it off Sarah, you'll find a way of coping. You're a strong girl." And she was, at least to the outside world.

***

Two weeks into classes, Sarah was finding the assignments daunting; even so, she worked hard keep up with it. Now she understood how her father had survived. Law was an extremely demanding field. All first year courses were automatically scheduled; she had no choice of subjects. It was obvious the weeding-out process began early. She wouldn't be weeded out, she promised herself.

Sarah had little contact with other students, and it was easy to lose herself in her work. She was more like her father than she'd thought.

Sitting in class, Sarah suddenly had a feeling she was being watched. Trying to be nonchalant, she dropped her pen and glanced around as she picked it up. Her eyes met a pair of sparkling dark eyes which belonged to an astonishingly handsome young man who had obviously been watching her. She looked away quickly, but could feel a blush creep up her face.

His face was imprinted on her mind. His skin was coffee-colored, his eyes and hair dark and shining. He had even features and very white teeth; he'd smiled at her. He was exotic looking and she found her heart racing. The rest of the lecture was lost on her. She was consumed with thoughts, *impure thoughts*, the nuns would've said, of this young man. She'd never had this reaction to a man before.

As class ended, Sarah took her time gathering her books, not looking up. As she stood, someone bumped into her. She looked up to see those same dark eyes, dancing with amusement.

"I'm so sorry!" the stranger said, not sounding the least bit sorry. He stooped to retrieve a book that had slipped from Sarah's grasp. Their hands brushed as he gave her the book. He never broke eye contact with her. "I'm Henrique Alvarez," he said offering his hand.

Flustered, Sarah croaked, "I'm Sarah Justice, nice to meet you."

Henrique laughed, "Your last name, I guess that's why you're in law school!"

"You've no idea!" Sarah replied, laughing.

"But I'd love to hear about it," Henrique said. "Are you free now? We could go for coffee."

Sarah had planned to go to the library, but that could wait, she decided. "Coffee sounds good!"

They walked to the nearest coffee shop, discussing random subjects along the way. Sarah detected a pronounced accent, Hispanic, she decided. It added to his charm when he misspoke or had difficulty finding the right word. She wondered if this would hamper his progress in law school.

Seated in the crowded coffee shop, Henrique opened the conversation. "I actually have a favor to ask of you," he said.

Sarah, curious, looked up. "What is it?"

"You might probably have notice, but I need to improve my English. I know you are very busy studying, I see how much you write in class. But do you have time to help me improve? I do understand if you cannot have the time."

He looked so vulnerable, so unaccustomed to asking for favors. *How could she say no?* "Of course I can find the time! There's only so much studying I can do before it makes me nuts, so sure, I'll help you out if I can. Maybe we can study together and do both." Sarah blushed as she realized what she'd said.

"That is so wonderful of you! You are most generous person!" Henrique picked up her hand and kissed it.

Sarah blushed again as erotic sensations coursed through her body. She had never, ever had a reaction like this from an encounter with any man. True, her experience was limited; she was choosy but she hadn't been captivated by any of the men she'd dated. This man oozed sex-appeal, and she had no defense. They sat and talked for a very long time. She found she could talk to him about anything, and she ended up telling her life story. Realizing she knew nothing about him, she said, "I'm sorry, I've monopolized the conversation. Please, tell me about you."

Henrique shrugged, "I'm not so interesting. I'm from Belize. I was raised by my aunt; my parents die in an accident when I was too young to know. My aunt, she was strict and much more old. When she die, she leave me enough money to travel. I always want to study the law, and I want to come to America. So, here I am!"

"Belize is said to be very beautiful," Sarah commented.

Henrique shrugged again, "Yes, and no. Very beautiful beaches and forests; It is a nice place for tourists, but to live there…"

"Not for you?" Sarah asked.

He nodded, "Exactly, yes, not for me. Not enough going on. America, she is so exciting! I love it here!"

"So, you plan to stay here?" Sarah asked.

"Yes! One hundred percent sure. I cannot leave now that I love it so much!"

Looking at her watch, Sarah realized two hours had gone by, and she'd accomplished none of her study goals for the morning. She almost laughed at herself. "Henrique, I have a class at two this afternoon, and was hoping to go home and study…"

"Can I walk you home?" Henrique offered. "I have class at same time, not same class as yours, but maybe we could study until then?"

"Sure, why not?" Sarah agreed. She led the way out of the coffee shop and they walked slowly to her apartment.

As they entered her apartment, Sarah tried to see it through Henrique's eyes. It was spacious and full of light. The furnished apartment, though not exactly her taste, was expensive and attractive. She had a full, eat-in kitchen, a large living room, a laundry nook and two bedrooms, each with its own bath. There were sliding doors out to a generous balcony, which had two chairs, a table and a grill. She kept the place neat, because she didn't do much besides study and eat here. Her father was paying the bill and he insisted on the best for her, *as long as it required just money,* she thought.

Henrique looked around and nodded. "Very nice place, like I would expect."

"What do you mean?" Sarah asked.

"You are very classy girl, and your place, it is also." Henrique answered. "And your father, the judge, does he pay for this?"

"He pays for this, yes," Sarah said, worrying she'd told him too much already. "But I've earned my own money too. I worked at the Stock Exchange the year after college."

"That must be very good job!" Henrique said, smiling.

"It was," Sarah conceded, "but not really for me. I just did it to save money."

Henrique changed the subject. "And your place, it is so neat. Because you study all the time?"

Of course, he was right, Sarah acknowledged to herself. She usually studied at the large desk in her bedroom, but that wouldn't do. She dumped her books on the kitchen table. "We can study here," she said. "Can I get you something before we start?"

"Just water, if you don't mind," Henrique answered.

Sarah got two bottles from the fridge, handed one to Henrique and sat down to study.

She pulled out her "Judicial Procedure" book for her afternoon class and began to read. She glanced up and saw Henrique had his nose in a different book, "Tort Law." That was a very boring class, she thought.

Sarah was unable to concentrate with Henrique sitting across from her. He seemed to be doing fine, or faking it, but her thoughts would not settle. He was unsettling. The rational part of Sarah's brain was sending warning signals, reminding her she needed to keep up her studies or be "weeded out." That was an outcome she couldn't accept. She would have to find time to study without Henrique.

They didn't talk much as they each read their assignments. Sarah finally settled enough to take in the basics of the text. She glanced up at her wall clock and said, "Oops! Time to go, I hardly noticed."

"Ok," Henrique agreed. "Let's get going. I think your class is farther than mine, yes?"

"I don't know," Sarah replied, flustered. "Where is your class?"

"Same as this morning," he said. "Should I walk you to your class first?"

"No, that's not necessary," Sarah said, as they walked outside. "See you later." She walked on ahead.

"I meet you after your class, no?" Henrique asked.

"Yes, fine, I'm done at 4:30," Sarah said quickening her step.

"I know," he said smiling. ""Please call me Henri, it is more easy."

"OK, Henri," Sarah replied as she walked even faster.

***

Sarah's head was swimming as she hurried to class. She was flattered beyond belief. He actually knew where her class was, and when it was over. How was it she'd never noticed him, and he knew so much about her. The answer was obvious; she'd had her head in one book or another ever since school started. She'd been oblivious to what was going on around her. She had made no new friends, with the exception of learning the names of two women who lived in her apartment building. She could hardly consider them "friends."

Arriving at class, just on time, Sarah took a seat near the front. She had decided to try her best to pay attention and put "Henri" out of her thoughts for the time being.

The class was hardly entertaining. It did not grab her interest. She took fewer notes than usual and found her thoughts wandering to Henrique. She checked the clock to see how much longer until she would see him, and sighed audibly.

The professor stopped lecturing and looked directly at her. "I'm sorry if you find this boring, Ms. Justice…"

Humiliated, Sarah mumbled, "I'm sorry Dr. Henson, I'm just tired." She blushed to the roots of her hair.

"Up late studying, no doubt," he commented, as he arched an eyebrow.

She decided instantly he was her adversary. How dare he call her out! He was boring as shit. She would ace this course and give him no reason to make an example of her in class. She knew he would be reading her briefs more critically, and she could ill afford any black marks on her record.

She began taking notes furiously. But, God, he was fucking boring!

***

True to his word, Henrique was waiting for Sarah as she emerged from the building.

"What took you so long?" Henrique asked. "You are the last one out." He sounded annoyed.

"The prof called me out in class because I yawned, and then he wanted to talk to me after class. He's an ass. I hate him!"

Henrique's eyebrows lifted. "Wow! He must be bad, you are such good student. Why do he treat you like this?"

"I guess he could tell I was bored, when I looked at the clock. But, Henri, he is sooo boring! The problem is, I think he has targeted me and now he will look very carefully at my work," Sarah said.

"What means 'targeted?'" Henri asked, frowning.

"It means he will single me out now and look for any mistakes, but I'm ahead of him there; I won't make mistakes." Sarah said stubbornly.

"You can do it, too, I'm very sure!" Henri said, smiling. "Now, let's get some dinner before study time." He led Sarah to a café popular with law students.

Before she knew it, Sarah was seated across from Henri and they were looking at a menu. He ordered a beer and asked what she wanted to drink. "Just water," she said.

"Oh, come on, you need something to relax, you had a bad day," Henri said.

"And it will be a worse day tomorrow if I drink tonight and 'forget' to study," Sarah answered.

"Just one little drink?" Henri teased. Sarah thought about how rigid she must seem to him. He was probably right, she'd been working so hard for the past few weeks. She hadn't once stopped to have fun. Here was her chance.

"Ok," Sarah said before she could change her mind, "I'll have a glass of Pinot Grigio."

Henri smiled, "That's my girl. You can have fun and study, too."

After one glass of Pinot, Sarah felt giddy and happy. She realized it had been quite awhile since she'd had alcohol and she'd never tolerated it particularly well. But she enjoyed the happy feeling.

***

The next morning, Sarah awoke naked in her bed, with a pounding headache and very little memory of last night's events. She was horrified and wondered how she'd allowed herself this lapse.

Sarah checked herself out and noticed faint bruising on her breasts and discomfort in her vagina. She wondered if she'd fallen, and the glaring question *was what happened last night?* Alarmed by noise in the kitchen, she grabbed her robe and threw it on.

Just then a smiling Henri came into her room with a steaming cup of coffee. "Here you are, you take only milk, right?"

"Right," Sarah stuttered as she accepted the coffee. Then she asked, "Henri, why are you here? What happened last night?"

"Calm down," Henri said. "Nothing happen. You just drink too much and I help you home. You fell few times. Then you got sick, so I have to take the nasty clothes off and I wash them," he said proudly. "I sleep in the other room, but I listen to see if you are sick again. My poor Sarah, you must feel bad." He brushed his hand over her face.

"I do feel bad, and I didn't get any studying done. I still have to write that brief for Professor Henson and he won't cut me any slack. I don't have morning classes, thank God, but I'll have to work the rest of the day. I'm sorry if I seem bitchy, Henri, but I have to get my work done."

"First I make you breakfast, and then I leave you to study, ok?"

"That would be lovely, Henri. Right now, I need a shower."

"Ok, you go ahead, breakfast will be ready when you get out," Henri assured her.

Sarah took her time in the shower, trying to clear her head and checking out her body. Henri had said "nothing happen," but was that true? It looked as if she had chafed breasts, and there was some soreness in her vagina. Maybe she was imagining it all, she just didn't remember. She hated not knowing, being out of control. She knew she couldn't drink much alcohol, so why had she done it? How much had she had? She just couldn't remember, that was the worst feeling. And she was too embarrassed to ask Henri, my God, she'd just met him and he already knew everything about her, including how she looked naked. She couldn't live like this; she had to get back in control.

Sarah took her seat in the kitchen, fully dressed, her hair clean and dried. Henri had made scrambled eggs, bacon and toast. He seemed at home in her kitchen. There were two aspirin next to her orange juice and she took them immediately. "You thought of everything, Henri, thank you."

"You are very welcome. I try to make up to you from last night. I didn't know you couldn't drink much. I think you had only two, maybe three glasses of wine," Henri apologized.

"Well, two or three are too many. I haven't had wine for quite awhile and I know how much I can drink. I'm sorry to have put you through all the trouble." Sarah replied.

"It was no trouble to me, I am just sorry for how you feel," Henri said. "Now, eat some breakfast and then you feel better."

After breakfast, Henri cleared the table, put the dishes in the dish washer, and took his leave.

"Here is my cell number, if you need me. I must go to class. Feel better!" Henri called out as he left.

Sarah put her pounding head in her hands and just sat for a moment. She had a feeling of dread, not being able to remember last evening. Henri had been so sweet, feeding her and treating her with kindness. She wondered if she would see him again, or if she had disgraced herself. She really couldn't afford lapses like this. Law school had to come first.

For the remainder of the morning, Sarah poured over her notes and the text. Her mind was working slowly and she fought to keep her focus. Like the professor's lectures, the text and notes were hardly exciting.

Sarah got up for water, and chugged a bottle straight down. She knew she needed to hydrate and remove the toxins from her body.

Getting back to work she felt marginally better, and she kept a bottle of water by her side, sipping frequently. She finished her first draft and decided she was ready to tackle the final. She was feeling more like herself, and she needed to ace this paper. Sarah looked at the clock; two hours to go. She could do this.

Sarah pulled the last page from her printer as she got ready to go to class. Having skipped lunch, she took two more aspirin, grabbed a few power bars and more water. Sarah ran out the door, backpack in her hand. She stopped short when she spotted Henrique.

He was waiting on the sidewalk. Her reaction was visceral. Thoughts of class evaporated; apparently he hadn't been repelled by her behavior last night.

"Feeling better?" he asked, taking her backpack and hefting it over his shoulder.

"Much better, thank you. It was so nice of you to make breakfast and wash my clothes! I got my work done after all. I hope it passes muster."

Henri cocked his head and looked confused.

"Oh, another expression. It means I hope the prof approves of it, and better than that, gives me the 'A' I deserve!"

"I hope so, too," Henri said. "I just had my first quiz in 'Legal Methods,' and I was ok, but not an 'A' I think. Maybe you teach me to do best work, like you?" Henri asked.

"I think you'll do just fine once you get the language down," Sarah replied. "You'll have to find your own best way of studying. I read everything over and over again. And, as you noticed, I take lots of notes."

Henri nodded. "Well, here is your class. Good luck! I see you after class?"

"Oh Henri, I don't think so; I have so much work to do," Sarah answered with regret.

"But, is Friday, you have all weekend to work!" Henri pleaded.

"I have an early Saturday class," Sarah answered. Then, seeing the look of disappointment on his face, she relented. "Ok, we can stop for a quick pizza, but no drinks for me!"

His dazzling smile returned. "Wonderful! I be right here after class."

Sarah had to shake herself mentally to push thoughts of Henri to the background, as she entered class.

***

True to his word, Henri was waiting outside after Sarah's class.

"Hi, how was it? Was he mean to you today?" Henri inquired.

"Well, I sort of hid in the back today. I don't think I'll sit in the front row again. I turned in my paper after class. Have to wait and see how I did," Sarah answered.

"I think you will get your Ace from the professor," Henri predicted, smiling.

"We'll see. I'm not sure he's forgiven me, he may be vindictive," Sarah replied. Then, seeing the questioning look on Henri's face, she said, "Vindictive means getting back at someone."

"Ah," he said. "That I understand."

They had reached the closest pizza shop. Entering first, Sarah said, "I'm starved!"

They ordered a pizza to share and found seats.

"So how was your morning class?" Sarah asked

Henri shrugged, "Not so bad," he answered. "It's the most interesting class I take. Not like 'Tort,' which I hate most bad. Half the time I even stop listening in that class, I am so confused."

"You might want to think about getting a small digital recorder, so you can record your classes and listen to them later. That's what I do with my notes, I just keep writing and try to make sense of it later," Sarah advised. "That would help with your English, too," Sarah added.

"That's why you are good student, well, and you smart, very smart, I think. I will try anything you say will help!"

When their number was called, Sarah jumped up to get it, as Henri protested.

"This is my treat, Henri, you've done your share of paying."

When Sarah came back with the pizza, Henri thanked her and then said, "In my country it is only weak men who let their women pay for them."

"Welcome to America!" Sarah said. "Women are equal here, well, not quite, but many women are the bread-winners in their families. That means they earn more money than their husbands. Also, some men stay home with the children."

A look of distaste came over Henri's face. "I have notice this sometimes, but is very difficult to accept."

"I imagine it is," Sarah agreed. "There are many men here who think like you. But my opinion is it's to men's advantage for women to share the burden, financial and otherwise, with each other."

"I will think about it," Henri said. "But what I grew up believing was so very much different.

***

After dinner, Sarah and Henrique strolled at a leisurely pace, enjoying the mild, Indian summer breeze. As they came closer to her apartment, Sarah struggled with the idea of telling Henri she needed some "alone time" to prepare for tomorrow's early class. Somehow she expected a push-back.

Arriving at her apartment, Henri said, "Ok if I come in and just stay for maybe a few minutes? I know you have class tomorrow." He gave Sarah another dazzling smile. And Sarah's earlier resolve evaporated, just like that. But, she would hold him to "a few minutes."

***

Several hours later, Sarah found herself almost literally pushing Henri out the door. They'd sat down to chat about their day and time passed quickly. Whenever Sarah brought up her class and the preparation she needed to do, Henri would find some charming way around it.

At nine o'clock, Sarah finally stood up saying, "And now, Henri, I really have to get some studying done." She walked towards the door and he followed like a chastened puppy dog. Once at the door, Henri pulled her into his arms and engaged her in a passionate kiss. Then he nibbled on her lips, and asked, "Do I really have to go? I so much enjoy you."

Sarah sighed, "I don't want you to leave, either, but it's very hard for me to concentrate on my work. You're a distraction, a lovely one to be sure. But I start feeling restless and guilty about not doing my work."

Henri looked sad, then brightened, "Just one more kiss?"

That one more kiss took on a life of its own, and was about to become something much more, when Sarah, gasping for air, pushed back. She wasn't ready for this. "Good night, Henri," she said firmly.

He took her hand and kissed it. "Good night, my lovely Sarah. Sleep well," he added, managing to make it sound like an invitation.

After he'd left, Sarah stood leaning against the closed door, wanting to call him back and knowing she couldn't. Things were moving so fast her head was spinning. She wondered how long it would be before she just caved. She took inventory of her disheveled clothes. Her bra was pushed up, her blouse undone, and this had taken place in mere minutes. Her body tingled and she longed for more.

She decided to take a shower before she tackled her studies. Stripping down, she entered the shower and turned knobs until she'd gotten the right temperature. As she used her hands to spread the shower gel, she found herself caressing areas of her body that had been stimulated. Before long, without intending to, she'd brought herself to climax, an image of Henri in her mind. It felt so good.

Her common sense was warring with her passion. No man had ever moved her so. She'd had sex, to be sure, but nothing beyond "ho-hum." Sarah had always figured sex was over-rated. She knew having sex with Henri would reel her in completely. She needed some distance, some time to sort things out and get back into her studies.

Sarah turned the water temperature to cold, hoping to douse the flame that had overtaken her. When the cold became unbearable, she quickly got out and dried herself. She dressed in her night clothes and went to her desk to study.

Her Saturday class was "Civil Procedure" and she'd always found it interesting. Right now it was running a distant second behind Henrique. She shook her head, trying to find her "study brain" and the discipline that had always come so easily. It had been her hallmark and she was shocked it could disappear so quickly. Henrique had a hold on her; he was a magnet.

Dragging her attention back to studying, Sarah hit the books with a vengeance. She gave it a full hour and a half before deciding she was done. She wondered if she'd overdone studying before, if maybe she could get by with less. She would have to see.

Still restless, Sarah decided to call her best friend, Lisa. It was nearly eleven, but Sarah expected Lisa would still be up. Lisa was in her second year of law school, at Harvard.

Lisa answered on the second ring, "Sarah! My God, how are you? Honestly, I was just thinking of calling you, but you go to bed earlier than me, usually. What's up?"

Sarah went on to describe the last few days' events to Lisa, with special emphasis on Henrique and his hold on her.

"Sounds like you finally met a real man," Lisa laughed. "I guess you'll figure out how to make it work with your first year of law school. You don't need to tell me, I know first year's a bitch!"

"You got that right! For the first two weeks, I worked my ass off, barely spoke to anyone, and kept my head in books. It will be a huge challenge to juggle school and a relationship," Sarah said.

"You'll come to your senses. You're a hell of a good student, and your studies have always come first. I guess you can't underestimate 'Latin lovers,' so maybe what they say is true." Lisa chuckled.

"Well, we're not lovers, technically," Sarah said. "But this guy, oh my God! Sorry to go all gaga on you, what's up at your end?"

"Well, I just met a honey of a guy, his name is Rob. He works in NYC, as a hedge-fund manager. Actually, I met him through my parents. I went to the city to meet them for dinner. He came into the restaurant, and my dad knows him so he introduced us. Talk about tall, dark and handsome, Rob fits the bill; he's gorgeous. And he wasted no time getting in touch with me. He came up to Cambridge last weekend and we had a marvelous time."

"So you have some idea of how to manage school and a lover?" Sarah asked.

"Whoa, we're not lovers, not yet anyway, but only because he's shown restraint. If it were up to me..."

"That's why I assumed you were lovers, you're not one to hold back. And that's not a judgement, by the way. I wish I could be more free, but I guess that's a side of myself I'm learning about."

Lisa laughed, then said, "I should let you off the hook, knowing you have to get up for an early class. But we have to plan a getaway soon; that is if you can bear to leave Henrique. Love you, Bye."

"Love you, too, Bye Lise." Sarah yawned, hoping she could go to sleep. That eight o'clock class tomorrow would come up quick.

***

Sarah dragged herself out of bed when the alarm went off at seven a.m. Her first impulse was to take a shower, but remembering last night's shower, she vetoed that idea. She took time to eat a good breakfast, had a cup of coffee, made one to go, and she was ready.

She checked her backpack to make sure she had everything, grabbed a bottle of water from the fridge, and was out the door.

Looking around, she was momentarily disappointed not to see Henri. But it was, after all Saturday, and very early. This was probably better, she decided. She knew she needed time and space.

Sarah had not walked very far, when she heard the pounding of running feet behind her. She moved over to make room for the jogger and was stunned to see Henrique slowing to a walk.

"So glad I caught you," he said, panting from exertion. "I could not sleep, I think of you all night!" He grabbed her hand and kissed it, an expression that had become endearing. Then he took her backpack.

Sarah just shook her head smiling, "So you couldn't sleep all night and you got up at this ungodly hour? That's crazy!"

"That's why they call it 'crazy in love,' no?" Again the dazzling smile.

"I guess it must be," Sarah replied, feeling somewhat uncomfortable.

"Look, I need to get moving, so why don't you go home and get some sleep; it's Saturday, you can sleep in," Sarah said, trying to set some boundaries.

"I walk you to class, then I go home," Henrique answered, matching her stride. He took her hand and held it as they walked.

Arriving at her building, Henrique released her hand and gave over her backpack. Before Sarah could thank him, he pulled her into an embrace and kissed her with great passion, leaving her breathless and tingling.

"Wow!" Sarah said, "I guess I'm wide awake now." She giggled like a schoolgirl, and bade him "Goodbye."

"I will see you later, no? For dinner?" Henrique asked.

"How about I make you dinner?" Sarah said without thinking.

"That is wonderful! What time I should come?" Henri asked.

"Around six is good, ok?" Sarah asked

"Sure thing, see you then my lovely Sarah." He blew her a kiss.

Maybe Lisa was right Sarah thought, there was *something* about Latin lovers. She knew her cover had been blown. She literally skipped to her building.

***

After class, Sarah was actually relieved Henri wasn't there to greet her. She'd bought herself some time for studying before dinner. She'd make something simple, like filet mignon. That was sort of macho, like him. They could grill outside on her balcony. She'd have to check the grill to see if it was operable, she hadn't used it yet.

She stopped at the grocery store nearest home and bought what she needed for dinner. She almost went into the liquor store, but stopped herself in time. Sarah could ill afford to have a repeat of that notorious first night. She blushed just thinking about it.

As she entered her building, she saw one of the women she knew, and said, "Hi Rita, how are you? How's school going?"

"It's kicking my ass, actually! I guess it's my fault, because I've met a guy I really like and I'm spending less time studying," Rita replied.

"Really?" Sarah said. "Why don't you stop over and we'll talk, it may be a common problem."

"Sounds good. I'm on my way out, be back in about an hour, ok?" Rita replied.

"Great, see you then," Sarah answered.

How nice, she thought, to have someone to share her problems with. They could support each other.

She set about preparing the meal and noticed that she'd bought more than she needed for one meal. Perhaps Rita and her friend could join them. That might be fun and less intense than her meetings with Henri had been. Sarah felt she was losing her perspective because Henri had become an almost constant companion. It seemed he wanted to spend every possible moment with her. And while it was flattering, it could be suffocating. When she was with him, his charm always won her over and his personality was dominant. And it was all happening so quickly!

As she was contemplating what to have for dessert, there was a knock at her door. Looking out, she saw it was Rita and opened the door.

"Hi, come in," Sarah invited.

"I was intrigued by what you said about a 'common problem,' and I have seen you with one handsome devil lately, so I assume we do have something in common. I met James the first week of school and I've been so smitten I can't seem to do any quality work," Rita said.

"Yes, I understand. But I just started seeing Henri a few days ago, and he seems to be consuming most of my time, even when he's not here. I've always been a serious student with tons of discipline, but it's disappeared in a flash," Sarah replied.

"Same story!" Rita said. "Or remarkably similar. So, what do we do about it?"

"For starters, would you and James like to come for dinner tonight? I have plenty of food and it might help decrease the intensity if we team up. What do you think?" Sarah asked.

"Great idea! Of course James and I were planning to spend the evening together, so it will be a treat to join you. I have a dessert already made, well, actually Trader Joe's made it, but I could bring that."

"Awesome! That's the only part I hadn't planned. We're grilling filet mignon, is that ok? Either of you a veg?" Sarah asked.

"Well, we don't usually eat red meat, but we always make an exception for the best red meat!" Rita answered.

"Me too," Sarah said. "I figured Henri to be a major carnivore, so decided on filet."

"Listen," Rita said, "we should make a pact to help each other out when we feel the need for study time or just solo time. Let's trade cell numbers so we can stay in touch."

"Great idea, I love it! Man, you came along at the right time." Sarah gave Rita a spontaneous hug.

Smiling, Rita said, "Now I think it's time to leave so we don't defeat our purpose. What time for dinner?"

"I told Henri six, but I'm sure he'll arrive early. By the way, I'm not serving alcohol because of our first disastrous night when I got roaring drunk and don't remember a thing. But feel free to bring alcohol if you want it," Sarah said.

Rita gave a rueful smile, "That's a relief. We don't drink because James is in AA and I respect that. I don't miss it; alcohol has fucked with my life too much already. My mom is an alcoholic, but she's twelve years sober now. It makes all the difference in the world!"

"Oh, that's got to be rough, but how wonderful you have her back!" Sarah's lip trembled as she said, "My mom died twelve years ago and I still miss her so much!"

Rita gave Sarah a hug, saying, "You only get one mom."

"But, I've been lucky," Sarah brightened. "I met a girl in boarding school who took me home with her all the time and they seem to have adopted me. They're lovely people."

"So you did get another mom, I'm happy for you."

"Ok, enough bloodletting!" Sarah joked. "See you and James tonight at six."

"With dessert," Rita added, "Bye."

Sarah sighed as she closed the door. She realized how much she'd missed having a friend.

Looking at the clock, Sarah said to herself, *and I have plenty of time for study.*

Her cell buzzed as if in rebuttal. She looked at the caller ID. It was Henrique and she chose not to pick up. Then she turned her cell off and went to her room to study.

***

Sarah was about to wrap up her studying when the buzzer from the entrance door sounded, not once, not twice, but repeatedly. She glanced at her watch and saw it was just five o'clock. Going to the window she looked out to see an angry Henrique, pushing the buzzer furiously. A bit put-out herself, she went to the door and pushed the button to unlock the main door.

She heard Henrique stomp up the steps and steeled herself for a blow-up. She opened the door before he knocked.

"Why have you not answered your phone?" he shouted. "I call and call you and no answer. I worry something has happened to you!"

Sarah answered coolly, "It's plugged in, charging. And I always turn it off when I'm studying. What did you need to know that was so important?"

"I, I just want to talk to you, check on the time," he said.

"But, it wasn't hugely important, right?' Sarah asked.

"You are important to me and when I can't reach you, I worry." He shrugged.

"Henri, a week ago you didn't know me and I guess you were fine. What's different now?"

"You have to ask?" Henrique sounded hurt. "I have met you and that makes all the difference. Now, can we drop the argument and get on with our evening?" He handed her a bottle of red wine.

Sarah grimaced. "Thanks for bringing the wine, Henri, but our first encounter, when I drank, was disastrous."

"Not for me it wasn't, I take care of you," he said.

And to herself, she thought, *Yeah, I bet you did*! She wondered again what had actually happened that night. She'd pushed those questions aside but they hadn't disappeared.

"Well, in any case, we can't drink tonight because I've invited a friend from the building for dinner and her boyfriend is in AA." Sarah said in a rush.

"You invited people I don't know, and now we don't have the evening alone, together?" He seemed to be barely concealing his rage.

"I ran into Rita in the hallway and we started talking. She, and her boyfriend, James are in law school, too, so I thought it might be nice; we all have that in common. Plus, I bought more food than we could eat, so I just made the decision. Sorry to have offended you. Now, since you're here an hour early, please make yourself useful. Could you check to see there's gas in the grill while I get a shower?" She walked to the bathroom, feeling proud she'd finally stood up to him.

He didn't answer, but she could guess that he was pissed as she heard him slide the door to the balcony open with more force that necessary.

Sarah hurried through her shower and was toweling herself dry when Henri walked in. He strode over to her embracing her, covering her mouth with kisses. The towel dropped, or was pushed off and soon Henri was exploring and nuzzling every part of her body. Her anger with him disappeared and she was overcome with passion. She nearly climaxed as he slid his fingers into the hot, moist place between her legs.

She pushed him away as the part of her brain still capable of rational thought said *STOP!*

"Henri," she said breathlessly, "our guests will be here in twenty minutes! And I still have dinner preparation to finish."

"Fuck them!" he said as he grabbed for Sarah.

She moved out of his reach, picked up her towel and covered herself.

Henri turned to leave the bathroom, then said, "You know, you can be cold bitch sometimes!" He slammed the door.

Sarah's feeling of arousal quickly evaporated. He'd shown his anger twice in a very short time. Alarm bells rang in Sarah's head and she was glad she'd invited Rita and James. She felt she'd reached a turning point and was glad she'd stood up to him.

Dressed and ready to finish meal prep, Sarah went into the kitchen. She didn't see Henri and didn't look for him as she got salad ingredients from the fridge.

Soundlessly, Henri came up behind her and put his arms around her, touching her breasts, and sliding his hands down her body.

As the vegetables dropped to the counter, Sarah struggled to turn around and confront Henri. He took the opportunity to give her another long, passionate kiss. Then he looked at her and said, "I am very sorry for what I said, it was not nice. Forgive me?" he asked, turning his puppy-dog eyes on her.

"Of course," Sarah said. "But, Henri, we need to find a way to have our 'fun' and also do our work. I cannot flunk out of law school. And I need to have other friends. I can't afford to have my entire social life revolve around you."

"You're right, I see, but when I'm around you, I just want to touch you all the time."

"I've noticed," she said drily, "but too much passion, too soon can burn out a relationship."

The ringing of the doorbell stopped their discussion. Sarah said to Henri, "Quick, hide the bottle!"

"No, I'm having wine. I don't give a shit if I'm the only one."

"Well, you will be," Sarah said over her shoulder as she went to answer the door.

She opened the door, smiling. Rita introduced her to James, who said, "Oh, I know you from Professor Henson's class."

Sarah frowned, "Oh dear, I guess you were there the other day when he called me out!"

"I was," James replied. "And I'm fairly certain the entire class applauded you for expressing what most of us felt. He is a bore-ass!"

"Thanks for saying that, James, but it was embarrassing."

Henri had come up behind Sarah, putting his arm possessively around her shoulder. She introduced him to Rita and James and he flashed his smile at them while shaking their hands.

"And I recognize you from Tort class," James said. "Another very boring class!"

"You can say that twice," Henrique replied.

***

The evening went well Sarah thought, but she was a bit miffed that Henri had downed the entire bottle of wine. The more he drank, the more charming he became and, curiously, the more fluent his English was. But she also worried that it might be difficult to get him to leave.

He surprised her after the couple left, by saying, "Well, I will go home now. I thought about what you said to me and I will try my part."

Sarah was happy to have him agree with her, but had to admit she was a tiny bit disappointed.

Of course, his leave-taking was passionate and long lasting. Sarah felt he was testing her, and as much as she wanted to let it run its inevitable course, she couldn't back down now or she would lose herself.

Regretfully, she pulled away, her clothes half-off and her hair disheveled. "Good night, Henri, thanks for being a good sport," Sarah said.

He smiled and said, "I can see you tomorrow for lunch?"

"That sounds good," Sarah said, "I do my best studying in the morning."

"Good, then we will spend the afternoon together?" Henri asked.

"Yes," said Sarah, "see you tomorrow."

Sarah was surprised that he left without, "one more little kiss." With Henrique, there was no such thing as a "little" kiss.

After cleaning the kitchen and turning the dishwasher on, Sarah decided she needed a cold shower before bed. It might help to cool her aroused state.

***

The next day, Henri arrived at noon, looking exceptionally handsome. He was in an expansive mood as he helped Sarah into a borrowed car and he told her they were going to Wilmington, the closest city to the law school.

Returning to the apartment after a lovely brunch at the Dupont Hotel in Wilmington, Sarah felt sleepy. "Henri, I need to take a nap, can we get together later?"

"You can have your nap and I will be no bother," Henri offered.

"How's that working?" Sarah asked.

"I sleep next to you and nothing happen, I promise."

Skeptical as she was, she relented, saying, "If you don't keep your word, out you go!"

Henri's face showed anger, but he answered, "OK, I behave."

Sarah left her clothes on and lay down on the bed. Henri lay down next to her, but not touching. Sarah was out like a light.

***

A few hours later, Sarah made waking noises and Henrique whispered in her ear, "Time to wake up my princess. It's five o'clock."

She turned towards Henri, ready for what came next. She received his kiss eagerly, a kiss that led the way to the inevitable. She'd known it was coming, why drag it on any longer?

They were both naked in minutes. Henri eagerly explored her as he'd never been able to do standing up with clothes on. Sarah was in ecstasy, all of her body throbbing with pleasure. She was ready.

Inexplicably, he stopped. Sarah looked up to see him, much to her relief, putting on a condom. *Jesus*, she thought to herself, she'd never seen a cock that big; no wonder he was always in heat. She hoped it would fit.

Sarah stifled a scream when he entered her; it hurt more than the first time she had sex. He pumped quickly, having an orgasm in a few minutes. Sarah was disappointed after all the build-up, and she was still in some pain.

"My wonderful Sarah, at last you are mine!" He brushed her lips with a kiss and said, "No worry, my sweet, we do this again soon." True to his word, they had sex several more times. Sarah watched the day turn to night outside her window.

Henri left without a fuss or "one little kiss," shortly after nightfall. Apparently he was sated for the moment.

Sarah pondered their "sex-athon" and found the experience was somewhat lacking. Unlike the foreplay, which had driven her crazy, culmination of the sex act was a disappointment. It made her think of the saying, "Wham-bam thank you ma'am."

She wondered if the thrill was gone; she hoped not.

***

The next morning, Henrique was not outside waiting for her. That was fine with Sarah, it freed her a bit. Then she wondered if she'd been just another "conquest" to him. That idea troubled her. She hated "users." Had she been used? Sarah shook her head, deciding to let it go. There were things about the relationship that had started to grate on her. She was afraid if she thought about it too much the relationship would soon end. She wondered, *Am I ready for that?*

Sarah noticed that Henri was not in class today. It freed her somewhat and she threw herself into Contract Law, taking plenty of notes. This was actually a good class, and the professor was obviously interested in this aspect of law. The professor's enthusiasm kept the students engaged.

After class, with no appearance from Henri, Sarah went to the library and studied as she ate her lunch outside, seated on a bench. Henson's class was next and she might get her paper back. She was anxious. She would soon know how he judged her brief.

Sarah got up and walked the short distance to Professor Henson's class. She sat closer to the front this time and vowed to take more notes. The professor lectured the whole time, not mentioning the papers.

With five minutes left, Sarah had covertly glanced at her watch, Henson ended the lecture. He said, "And now what you've all been waiting for..." He pulled the papers out of his desk with a flourish, and started calling names. Sarah, near the middle of the alphabet, got up to receive her paper when her name was called. She hated that her knees were knocking. She took the paper and turned to leave the room. Stopping at the back of the room, Sarah glanced at the last page. "B-" is what she saw. Tears of anger and frustration sprang to her eyes. Then she read the comment. It said, "You have much potential, Sarah. This is not your best work."

Ready to defend herself, she stopped and read it again. She actually knew this was not her best work. It couldn't have been given the time she took to write it and the condition she was in at the time.

As the last student left, Sarah walked up to the professor. He looked up, registering surprise. "Dr. Henson, I want to thank you for your comment. I'm not happy about the grade, but you're right, I can do better."

"Thank you, Sarah, for taking the comment as it was intended. It was a fine paper, and for some students, it might've been an "A," but not for you. You are capable of much more and I look forward to seeing that work."

Both the professor and Sarah were smiling when she left the room. She was resolved to return to her disciplined study. Her happiness was short-lived because an angry Henrique waited outside on the pavement. "Why you always are late from this class?" Henri demanded. "I think you like the professor!"

Sarah sighed at the childish antics. "I like him better than I did last week. I got a B minus on the paper, and I deserved it. I took my eye off the ball, it wasn't my best work. So I told Henson I appreciated his comment, but wasn't happy with the grade. We ended on a good note."

Henri didn't answer right away, then he asked, "So, you are now what they call a 'brown nose?' What is so wrong with a B-minus? I think is good grade."

"No, I'm not a 'brown noser;' I'm a serious student. Besides, It's not really the grade that counts, it's just that I could've done better. I know that and Henson said the same thing."

"So now you two 'lovey-dovey,' is that it?" Henri demanded.

"He's my *professor*, Henri, and he's old enough to be my father!" Sarah explained as if she were talking to a child.

"You never know, these old guys want a little piece of a beautiful young thing."

"I hope you're kidding, Henri, because that's a disgusting thought," Sarah said, turning on her heel and walking away.

Catching up with Sarah, he grabbed her arm and took her hand. "I'm sorry if I got you angry. I was just worried when you didn't come out right away."

"Henri, you remember our talk? I said I needed to take school more seriously and we needed to make time for study first. Getting a lower grade than I usually get was the first sign that I'm not serious with my studies."

"Yes, I remember, so when can we see each other?" he asked.

"When we've finished our work. And it's too hard for me to study with you. As I said you are a distraction, not in a bad way," she added.

"OK, so what about today?" Henri asked.

"Today, I go back to my apartment and study for tomorrow's class," Sarah answered.

"But, tell me this, do we have time for dinner together?" he asked, giving his puppy-dog look.

The look had less effect, but Sarah relented anyway. "OK, let's stop by Subway."

They ordered sandwiches, but the place was crowded, so Sarah agreed they could eat at her apartment as long as Henri understood it was just to eat.

Of course he agreed readily, but Sarah began to wonder about the wisdom of her decision.

The weather had turned, so it was too cool to eat outside. They arrived at Sarah's and went in to eat. They chatted as they ate and Sarah asked something that had been on her mind. "Henri, your English has improved remarkably. Is that just from listening to my perfect English?" Her tone was sarcastic and not lost on Henri.

He had the sense to look chagrined. He shrugged, smiling and said, "I was desperate to get your attention, I'd been staring at you and trying to get you to look back. Well, it worked, but I'm happy to give up the pretense."

"Me too! Thank you for fessing up," Sarah said smiling.

"What means 'fessing up?'" he asked playfully.

Sarah laughed, then she said, "I was wondering why your English improved when you were drinking. That was the first clue."

They got up to clear away the clutter from their sandwiches.

"Sorry, but I have studying to do," Sarah said.

"I know," Henri said, "but I need just one little kiss."

Sarah knew what to expect and didn't feel like an argument.

As always, he pulled her close and drove her to distraction with his busy hands. Her jeans hit the floor and before she knew it he had lifted her to the kitchen table where he quickly thrust into her several times before ejaculating.

Sarah pushed away, horrified, "Henri, you didn't use a condom! This will not happen again!"

He appeared contrite as he helped her back into her clothes and kissed her gently. "I am so sorry. I promise you it won't happen again."

She shook her head, as if trying to make sense of what had just happened. Everything moved so quickly with him she didn't have time to think. She knew she would worry until she got her next period.

***

The weeks passed as the fall weather turned colder, the leaves falling. Sarah continued to see Henri. She'd been calling the shots, except for the "just one kiss," requests that were a nightly occurrence. He didn't seem to want to sleep over or to have leisurely sex; evidently he was happy with "quickies," and Sarah enjoyed the foreplay, such as it was. Since her ultimatum, he always used a condom,

Sarah had gotten her period on schedule. When she realized what a huge relief it was, she knew she could never consider having a child with this man. In many ways, he was still a child himself. She began to think of ways to cut her losses and get rid of him. She also had recurring doubts about their first night together, and she became almost certain that Henri had slipped her a drug. What else was he capable of?

Sometimes they ran into Rita and James and had meals with them, which was a nice diversion. Meeting in the hall one day, Rita asked to come in and talk. She seemed uneasy, and Sarah was curious what was on her mind. Perhaps a fight with James?

Rita stood uncertainly by the door, prompting Sarah to say, "Come in and have a seat. What's on your mind?" Rita sat, and seemed to be deciding what to say. Sarah waited.

"This may be none of my business, so please tell me to butt out if I'm over-stepping," Rita began.

"Please, go ahead," Sarah offered.

Rita began again, "I don't really know what understanding you and Henri have about exclusivity, but I think you should know he's been seen with other women on campus. James has seen him, and Henri asked James not to tell you. But James told me, so I felt the need…"

"I see," Sarah said with a sigh. "Well, thank you for telling me, really! It makes it easier to break it off. I've known for awhile it wasn't going anywhere. The 'charm' has worn off, and for all the sexiness he exudes, he doesn't back it up, if you know what I mean. It's all about him. So, I guess I'm not surprised that he's a cheater. But I would like to find a way to 'catch him in the act,' so to speak. Do you think James would be willing to help me out?"

"I'm sure he would," Rita said. "But he wouldn't want to be directly involved."

"Oh, I understand perfectly. All he needs to do is to let me know when and where I might see Henri with his pick of the week," Sarah said, warming up to the idea.

"Thank you, Rita, and thank James for being a stand-up guy. I think you've got yourself a catch there. Not too many guys will 'dime out' one of their own, so I'm guessing he's not a cheater."

Rita smiled, "I'm pretty happy with him, I don't think he's a cheater. Okay, I've got to run now. I'll talk to James and we'll get back to you."

"Thanks, Rita, Bye," she said as she ushered her to the door.

Her cell phone buzzed and she saw it was Henrique, almost as though he knew something was up. She ignored the call and instead called her best friend, Lisa.

Lisa answered right away and listened to Sarah's story. It was not an uncommon story. When Sarah had finished, Lisa said, "You're not crying, and in fact you seem fine. Am I right?"

Sarah realized that Lisa, as usual, was right. "Yes, you're right. I guess I just realized this is a relationship I'll be better off without. He won't leave without a fight, of that I'm sure; he has a real macho streak and is used to getting his way."

"You'll find a way out; you're smart. And while I have you, my parents want you to join us for Thanksgiving, how about it?" Lisa asked.

Tears formed in Sarah's eyes as she thought of her adopted family. Her father called her every week, but had not mentioned Thanksgiving. "That would be the most lovely thing, thank you! Tell your parents, 'yes,' I would like nothing better." Sarah was happy to have something to look forward to, and to get away from Henri.

***

Sarah didn't pick up any of the several calls she received from Henri and later that day she met with James and Rita and discussed places and times when Sarah might "catch" Henri with other women. Of course, most of the times coincided with Sarah's classes, but she decided she could afford to leave a class early, and she had to do it soon.

The very next day, she left a class early and strolled along the route Henri was supposed to take. She sat on a bench to wait. Soon, she spotted Henri and an attractive young woman long before he saw her. She noted he had his arm around her and their heads were close together. *Bingo. Sarah thought, Gotcha!*

As the couple approached their heads still together, Sarah stood up, blocking their path. Henri's look of annoyance turned to one of alarm, as he sputtered, "Let me explain…"

"No need, Henri, I think I can see what's going on here," Sarah said, her voice oozing scorn. She looked at the young woman who gave her a nasty look. "Good luck!" Sarah said and turned on her heel to leave. She was happy with the encounter, although she knew there'd be repercussions. She'd handled herself with dignity and had taken the first step out of this relationship. She walked back to her apartment as fast as she could.

Fumbling with her key when she reached her front door, Sarah turned to see Henri closing in on her. She got the key in the lock and virtually burst through the door, slamming it behind her.

It didn't take long for him to start pounding on the door. She raced up the steps to her apartment, stopping only when she got to her door. She immediately went to the locked drawer where she kept the gun her father had insisted she take. She knew how to use it and would, if she needed it.

As the pounding on the front door continued, Rita came out of her apartment. Rita knocked on Sarah's door and said loudly, "So I guess you did it?"

Sarah opened her door and motioned Rita into the apartment. She closed and double locked the door, still holding the gun. Then she went to look out the front window. Rita came to her side and looked out.

"Oh, God, he followed you here. Not giving up easily," Rita said. "Looks like trouble. I guess you're serious," Rita said, looking at the gun.

"Oh, yeah, I have to thank my father for insisting I have one. Henri is *big* trouble. You know how charming he can be?" Rita nodded. "Well the flip-side of that is ferocious anger."

Sarah dropped into a chair, exhausted.

"Do you care about him?" Rita asked.

"No, it's over. He was becoming a bad habit I can't afford. And your information made it easy."

They could still hear the pounding from downstairs. "Rita, are you expecting James?"

"Yes, in about a half-hour, why?"

"He has a car, right?" Rita nodded. "Can you ask him to meet us out back; we can go out the back entrance. And then I'll treat you guys to dinner. I just don't want to be here alone. I'll report him to the super and ask that he call the police if Henrique doesn't go away."

"Sure thing." Rita reached James directly and he agreed to the plan. She turned to Sarah, "He said of course he'd meet us in the back parking lot, in about fifteen minutes. He'll call us when he arrives so we don't have to wait around outside."

Sarah was on the phone with the superintendent of the building and reported the incident, then said to Rita, "Thanks, Rita, thanks so much! By the way, do you know anyone looking to share an apartment?"

"Well, actually I'm looking for something cheaper; I'm on a month to month lease at this point because I came for summer term. What do you have in mind?"

"I'd like a room-mate. Are you interested? I just don't know to what lengths Henri will go, but I'm afraid to be here on my own."

"How much rent would you charge?" Rita asked.

"Rita, I'll take whatever you can afford, but I don't really need the money, so let's keep it low. Or maybe we'll use what you would've paid for groceries. What do you think?"

"That would be a huge weight off my mind, Sarah," Rita said. "Thanks for the offer."

"And it goes without saying that James is welcome here whenever you want to see him. I just hope it doesn't get too scary for us with Henrique hanging around. Henri doesn't have a key that I know of, but I'm getting a deadbolt just as soon as I can."

James arrived a few minutes later. Sarah and Rita were waiting inside the back door, and ran out to the car as soon as he pulled up. "Thanks so much, James, for everything!" Sarah said, breathless. "Let's find some expensive, out-of-the-way place for dinner. My treat!"

***

Rita moved in that weekend and Sarah had a deadbolt installed. Sarah never went out alone; she soon developed a "posse" of friends and was escorted everywhere. Henri still called her, leaving messages of his heartbreak. And she often spotted him behind her, but she never let him get close.

***

Rita didn't go home for Thanksgiving, so she and James stayed in the apartment when Sarah was gone.

The Thanksgiving break was a balm for Sarah. She was with the people she loved most and they returned the love in words and deeds. She had time to think about the "affair" with Henrique. It left a very bad taste in her mouth.

Sarah and Lisa talked endlessly, and most of it was not about Henri, even though she was concerned that he wasn't through with her. Lisa was in probably the best relationship of her life. Rob had come for Thanksgiving dinner, and he was all Lisa had said he was.

When it was time to leave, Sarah cried. She hugged everyone and promised she would be back to visit. "And, Lisa, I'll let you know about Henri," she said as an aside.

***

As the cab pulled up to her apartment, Sarah's stomach knotted. On her doorstep sat Henrique. He was holding a small box. Before she got out of the cab, she called Rita and got an immediate answer. "I'm here and I'm hoping you are home. Henri's waiting for me, so please buzz me in!"

Henri came toward her and reached for her suitcase. He had his "sad puppy dog" face on. He was so predictable!

"I can carry it, Henri," she said harshly. "And you can keep your gift. If you come near me again, I'll get a restraining order. We're done!"

He grabbed her and shook her until she dropped her suitcase.

Sarah managed to pull away and took the gun from her pocket. "Maybe you understand this better!" she said with controlled anger as she pointed and cocked the pistol. "We. Are. Done!"

Henrique's eyes blazed with rage, but he backed off, hurling one last retort through gritted teeth, "Oh, no we're not, Princess! You will live to regret this!"

Sarah carefully released the hammer and placed the gun in her coat pocket. The door buzzed and she walked through shutting it and her relationship with Henrique firmly behind her.

THE END.

About the Author

Jacquelyn Bishop lives in Media, a charming small town, not far from Philadelphia.

Though her formal training, at the bachelor and masters levels was in social services, her life-long dream was to write. And, having written her first novel, Death Sentence, she continued with this, her second.

Writing is a full-time job, she's discovered, but she finds time for walking, yoga, Zumba, and quality time with her grand-daughter, Lilia, who, at six, is a very wise little person.

Travel also takes up a good deal of time, especially visiting with friends and family in California.

Ordering Information

Death Sentence by Jacki Bishop is available now at online booksellers.

Sarah's Gone Missing by Jacki Bishop is available now at online booksellers.

Seduction of Sarah by Jacki Bishop is available now at online booksellers.

To order additional copies of this and future books by Jacki Bishop, please use the contact information below:

Early Riser Publishing
P.O. Box 711
101 E. Baltimore Ave.
Media, PA 19063
www.JackiBishop.com
jaxstir@gmail.com

Thank you for reading this book. I would appreciate any and all reviews online. ~Jacki